D0524628

Animal Friends All Year Long

Welcome to RIVER BEND

Table of Contents

Miss Kitty's Surprise . 6

The Giddy Day 8

Kenny Pig's Store . . . 10

The Easter Tree 12

Hand-Me-Downs . . . 14

Proud Angelo 14

Summer Sounds 16

A Most Unusual
    Boat 16

Bumping Along
    Shady Lane 18

Homemade Teddy . . . 20

The Happy Bicycle . . 21

The Test 22

A Happy Day 24

The Big Parade 26

Too Hot To Play 28

The Walking Hat . . . 29

Castaways 30

Two-Family House . . 32

Harvest Day 34

Boo! 36

Fisherman's Luck . . . 38

First Snowfall 40

Lost and Found 42

The Unexpected
    Guest 43

Introduction

NOW, IF you were to ask me, "Where IS River Bend?" I would answer
you, truly, that it is very close to where I live. I visit there quite often.
Perhaps you've been there too.
The very first time I told my little boy about the village, and my friends
who live there, he said, "Oh, I've been there lots of times!"
Then he sat right down and drew a map to prove it. And that is just the
way you'll find it. For that's how Jonathan found it.   P.M.S.

Animal Friends All Year Long

Originally published under the title *The Golden Storybook of River Bend*

By Patricia Scarry

Illustrated by Tibor Gergely

MERRIGOLD PRESS • NEW YORK

© 1969 Merrigold Press, Racine, Wisconsin 53402. All rights reserved. Printed in the U.S.A. No part of this book may be reproduced or copied in any form without written permission from the publisher. All trademarks are the property of Merrigold Press. Library of Congress Catalog Card Number: 87-80082 ISBN: 0-307-10992-5
A B C D E F G H I J K L M

Miss Kitty's Surprise

FROM the old Stone Bridge along Shady Lane you can see where the river meets the sea. And close by the bridge lives Miss Kitty Cat, in a tiny house perched over the water.

Miss Kitty was busy writing names on envelopes. For tomorrow, she planned to have a party for all her friends in River Bend. Everything was ready, except for the invitations. All day long Miss Kitty had been icing chocolate brownies. Cider was chilling on the porch. And there were even gay paper streamers hanging over the table.

Miss Kitty nibbled her pen and tried to think of a name for her party. It wasn't a birthday party. And it wasn't a holiday. Now what kind of a party should it be?

Suddenly Miss Kitty heard a noise outside. Could it be Zippy Raccoon, the mailman, coming for her letters? Oh dear! And she hadn't written even one party invitation.

Miss Kitty opened the door. Well, what a surprise. There were all her friends climbing out of Father Bear's funny truck and climbing onto her porch.

"Hello, Miss Kitty!"

"Hello, Miss Kitty!"

"We've come to see you," called her friends.

Oh, Miss Kitty was simply delighted. She welcomed them into her warm little house. And then it was their turn to be surprised.

"Why, you're having a party, Miss Kitty!"

"Look at the streamers!"

"Smell the brownies! It's a SURPRISE PARTY!"

Soon everyone was blowing party horns and putting on gay paper hats. Then they all sat around Miss Kitty's table and ate her delicious brownies and drank cold cider. It was a glorious party. Everyone agreed nothing is quite as much fun as a surprise party.

As for Miss Kitty, she was the most pleased and surprised of all!

The Giddy Day

THE spring wind whooshed through the village. It was a Doing Day. Miss Kitty washed all of her sheets and hung them on the clothesline.

Rabbit left his house in the Brambles and climbed to the top of Big Meadow. He was carrying a magnificent kite that he had made himself.

The wind was in a mischievous mood. It picked up Rabbit's kite and slapped it to the ground. Rabbit held the tail of his kite and ran backwards to catch the wind.

WHOOSH! The wind picked up Rabbit's kite. Before he could let go, it picked up Rabbit too!

"Help!" cried Rabbit. But there was no one to hear him.

Up, up over the trees sailed Rabbit, clinging to his kite. His heart pounded wildly.

The wind blew him gently over Kenny Pig's store. Poor Rabbit began to worry. Where was he going to land? Down below, Kenny was throwing tomato cans at Rabbit's kite, trying to knock it down.

Then the wind lowered him over the village dump, where Angelo Squirrel was burning the

8

garbage. Rabbit shut his eyes and coughed in the smoke. When the wind picked him up again he was sooty-black, and sailing towards the river.

"Oh don't drop me in the river, please Wind!" begged Rabbit. He could see Miss Kitty waving from her porch. Then the wind grew tired of its game. It stopped blowing, and down, down, down fell Rabbit. Would he fall into the rushing river and be carried out to sea? He let go of the kite.

WHOOSH! He slapped into something damp and soft, and hung on tight.

Rabbit felt himself being pulled sideways. When he dared to open his eyes, he smiled, for there was dear Miss Kitty pulling him in on her clothesline. He had landed on one of her sheets!

Rabbit sat on her porch. He was very happy to be on the ground. Then Miss Kitty spread out the sheet and said,

"I think I'll make a curtain out of this!" For there in sooty black was the print of Rabbit, with his outflung paws, and his standing-up ears, on that big white sheet.

It looked so funny that even poor Rabbit had to laugh.

Kenny Pig's Store

KENNY PIG'S store was a nice place to visit. It smelled of gumdrops and tea and apples.

But oh! Kenny's store was dirty! The soup cans and cookie boxes were covered with dust. And you couldn't see the fruit inside the glass case because the glass was never washed.

One morning a noisy bumblebee flew inside Kenny's open door.

"Shoo!" said Kenny. He pulled off his apron and flapped it at the bumblebee, trying to chase it out the door.

Flap! went Kenny's apron, dusting off the soup cans. The bumblebee flew over to the cookie boxes. Flap! went Kenny's apron, dusting off the cookie boxes. Now that tease of a bee was hiding.

Kenny Pig could hear him buzzing somewhere. Maybe the bee had got into the fruit shelf. But Kenny couldn't see through the glass. He squirted some window cleaner on the glass, then he rubbed it clean with his apron. Now he could see all the fruit through the nice clean

"Well, that's good news, Miss Kitty," smiled Kenny, as he tied on his apron.

Miss Kitty looked around the store. She was amazed to see the fruit showing behind the clean glass. The dust was gone from the soup cans. Even the floor looked swept.

"Why, Kenny Pig, you've been cleaning!" said Miss Kitty. "Everything looks so beautiful."

Kenny smiled happily. Then Miss Kitty suddenly saw Kenny's apron. But she didn't say a thing about that, because she was very polite.

window. But he couldn't see the bumblebee.

"Buzzzz! Buzz!" Perhaps that bee was hiding in a corner on the floor. Kenny pulled a broom from the broom rack and banged it into a corner. Whoosh! How the dust flew! No bee there. He tried the next corner, and the next. Soon there was a big pile of dust in the middle of Kenny's store, so he swept it outside the door.

He put the broom away, just as Miss Kitty walked into the store and said, "Oooh! A big bumblebee just flew out of your store!"

The Easter Tree

Next to having parties, Miss Kitty loved best to tend her small garden by the river.

On Easter Saturday Rabbit found her there, planting a little tree.

"That tree won't grow, Miss Kitty," he said. "It hasn't a root."

Jonathan Mouse shook his head.

"That tree won't blossom unless you put water in the hole."

Rabbit made a nest of his clothes beside his bed. And in the night the Easter Bunny filled it with chocolate eggs.

Jonathan woke up on Easter Sunday and found his chocolate eggs in the sugar bowl, where the Easter Bunny always hid them.

Little Richard found a beautiful basket of eggs on his bedside table. Angelo Squirrel and

"It will blossom tomorrow," smiled Miss Kitty. "It's an Easter Tree."

"Well, I hope you won't be disappointed," said Rabbit.

"Come by tomorrow and you'll see," promised Miss Kitty. Then they all wished each other a Happy Easter, and went home to wait for the Easter Bunny.

Of course, everyone has his own way of doing things, especially in River Bend.

sent marshmallow chicks and candy eggs flying!

After breakfast everyone hurried to Miss Kitty Cat's house. For surely, her Easter Tree could not have bloomed overnight. But!

"Isn't it beautiful?" gasped Little Richard.

his family ran about the yard in pajamas, finding eggs hidden in the grass.

Poor Kenny Pig thought the Easter Bunny had forgotten him, until he bumped into his cash register. The drawer popped open and

"I can't believe my eyes," said Jonathan.

Miss Kitty looked as proud as could be. For her little tree had blossomed with chocolate eggs, all wrapped in paper and hanging from golden ribbons. It was a lovely sight to see.

"I knew it would blossom overnight," said Miss Kitty. "With the help of the Easter Bunny. It's an Easter Tree, you see."

13

Proud Angelo

THE little village of River Bend looke[d] lovely. Trees had burst into bloom, and wil[d] flowers nodded by the lane. It was time fo[r] sprucing up.

Father Bear was painting his barn. Jonatha[n] Mouse was building flower boxes. And every[-] one in town was hoping that Angelo Squirre[l] would soon begin fixing up his house.

Hand-Me-Downs

I'm all pinned up
In my big brother's clothes.
With a tuck in the cap
It won't sit on my nose.

The coat is so roomy
It could shelter two,
But we'll just move the buttons,
It'll fit me like new.

The trousers are flappy.
I can't see my feet.
But we'll tuck up the cuff
And hitch in the seat.

With a snip and a stitch
There'll be more of me showing.
In my big brother's clothes
We can tell that I'm growing!

Then one day a beautiful blue flower blossomed among the leaves. Then another, and another, until the shabby little house was covered with beautiful blue morning-glories. There wasn't a broken shutter to be seen, or a strip of peeling paint showing through. Angelo's house looked like a lovely bouquet, as blue and fresh as the sea.

While all his friends hammered and painted, lazy Angelo sat happily in the sun. He was very sure that his was the prettiest house in the village of River Bend.

Angelo's house, on Applesauce Lane, looked like something from his dump. The paint was peeling. The shutters dangled crazily. The windows were cracked. But none of his neighbors would dream of asking him to please fix his house, for that might hurt his feelings.

One day Jonathan Mouse saw Angelo digging a trench in front of his porch. The next day Miss Kitty saw him on a ladder stretching strings from the roof to the ground. Everyone hoped that Angelo was going to tie the shutters in place with the strings. But no.

He bought some packages of seed from Kenny Pig. He scattered them into the trench and covered them with earth. Then he sat in a broken chair, enjoying the sun, when he wasn't busy at the dump.

As the weeks passed, pretty green leaves climbed from the earth and up the strings. Up and up they climbed, all the way to the roof.

Summer Sounds

The sky is a-rustle
With the strum of wings.
The field is a-bustle
With buzzing things.
Crickets, bugs and bees all humming
Shrill a song of summer's coming!

A Most Unusual Boat

In the old boathouse near Miss Kitty's house Rabbit had been building a boat. One afternoon Jonathan said, "Well, Rabbit's boat is finished. He's going to put it in the river tomorrow."

"Hooray!" cheered Little Richard. "Does it have a powerful motor?"

"No. It hasn't a motor at all. It doesn't even have a sail," said Jonathan uncomfortably. "In fact, it only has one oar!"

"How odd! I can't wait to see it," said Miss Kitty.

"Rabbit said we could all ride in it tomorrow. But only if he's finished his costume and learned his songs," said Jonathan.

"Costume! Songs?" cried his friends.

"Yes, I'm afraid the poor chap's acting a bit peculiar," mumbled Jonathan.

The next day Rabbit's friends were waiting on the river bank as he punted his boat towards them. Oh it was beautiful!

"Is it a canoe?" called Little Richard. "No. It's called a gondola. I saw it in a picture book," said Rabbit. "And I'm a gondolier."

He certainly was! Rabbit paddled his long sleek boat to shore, and his friends climbed aboard. They admired his boat and his costume, too. For he was dressed in a beautiful sailor suit and a big straw hat. And as he pushed his single oar he sang the most romantic song.

His passengers clapped and cheered, "How grand! Simply elegant!"

Rabbit grinned jauntily and said, "I do add a bit of dash to the river, don't I?"

Bumping Along Shady Lane

ONE day Zippy did remember to empty the mailbox. He had just put all the letters into his mailsack when Father Bear's truck came racing along Shady Lane.

The truck was piled high with chicken crates. It hit a bump and CRASH! suddenly the air was filled with feathers and flapping wings and angry squawks.

His first stop was at Kenny Pig's store.

"I've got something for you, Ken," said Zippy, pulling open the mailsack.

"SQUAWK!" Out of the sack flew the lost hen!

Kenny was so surprised that he fell back into a tower of macaroni boxes.

Zippy was so startled that he fell into the flour sack.

Father Bear jumped out of the cab and raced to catch the hens. Zippy dropped his mailsack on the grass and ran to help him. At last they found nine frightened hens and put them inside the cab.

"Zippy, there's still one hen missing," said Father Bear.

"Well, I'll watch for her along the lane," promised Zippy, as Father Bear waved good-bye and drove home, with hens squawking about him.

As he cycled along Shady Lane with his mailsack on his bike, Zippy looked among the bushes for the lost hen.

The two friends sat up and began to laugh. Then Zippy laughed even harder when he saw a stream of grain trickling onto Kenny's head. For there was the lost hen, happily nibbling at a sack of grain above him.

"Tee hee hee!" giggled Kenny. "Now that's what I call a Surprise in the Mail!"

Homemade Teddy

He's not like any Teddy
That you'd buy downtown.
His coat was made from Grandaddy's
Old dressing-gown.
His eyes were once the buttons
On my Mommy's baby shoes,
And he's stuffed with an old pillow
That the sofa used to use.
His nose is to-one-sideish,
Just a little wooly lump,
But his mouth is always smiley
Even when he gets a bump.
He's my brother, I'm his Daddy.
I don't know, really, which,
But I love him. Grandma made him
With a kiss in every stitch.

The Happy Bicycle

Tick! Tick! Tick!
My bicycle sings
As I ride along the lane.
I pinned some paper
Inside my wheel
And I tick like a clock
  'Til I stop.
   Tick! Tick! Tick!
    And I'm off again.

The Test

SINCE his last accident, Jonathan had hammered the dents out of his car. Now he was going to test the anchor that Rabbit had made for him out of a rake and a long piece of rope.

Rabbit was busy tying the end of the rope to the seat of the car. Several friends had gathered to watch, for everyone had agreed that Jonathan must not be allowed to drive his car unless he could stop it.

Jonathan was very nervous. He hoped that the anchor would work, for he could not bear to give up driving his beloved little car.

"There, your anchor is all tied in," said Rabbit. "Good luck, Jonathan!"

"Thank you," replied Jonathan. Then he bent to turn the key in his car. But it would not turn at all! ˎ

When Jonathan turned the key in the other direction, the car let out a roar. But Jonathan was so pleased with himself, he forgot to leap into the seat.

VROOOM! The little car plunged forward without him!

"Oh!" cried Jonathan. And he began to run behind it.

Poor Jonathan ran as he had never run before, for he just *had* to catch up with his car!

He made a tremendous jump. He landed, with one paw over the back seat, and hung on desperately! At last he managed to climb into the speeding machine, and he found himself clutching the steering wheel, with his heart pounding wildly.

He was almost in front of Mr. Foxy's house. Much farther than he'd planned to drive. So he pulled the steering wheel around and headed back for Kenny's store where his friends were waiting anxiously. "And now for the big test!" he told himself.

In just a moment he would throw out the anchor and stop the car in front of his friends. He pulled hard on the steering wheel, just for courage...and it came right off in his paws!

Poor Jonathan! He was so nervous he didn't know what to do. Then he flung the steering wheel, good and hard.

"Look out!" shouted Kenny Pig. There was a crash of glass as the steering wheel sailed through the last window of Kenny's door.

Jonathan was so excited that he forgot where the anchor was. He felt for it on the floor of his car, where one of his shoes lay. He

"But it didn't work right away!" said Kenny Pig.

"Oh I just need a little practice," grinned Jonathan.

"And what about your poor head?" asked Miss Kitty.

"It's just fine," said Jonathan, trying not to feel the lump.

After the test, he spent every day learning to throw out his anchor. He would fling it at a log or a bush where it would hold fast. And soon he could stop his car anywhere.

Rabbit made him a little seat belt from an old elastic garter. That kept Jonathan safely in his seat. Jonathan wasn't a reckless driver any more. He was a happy mouse.

flung out his shoe. And then he saw the anchor lying on the seat.

Jonathan grabbed the rake and flung it. The rope sailed into the air. It landed on a tree stump and clung there. The rope pulled firm, and jolted the little car to a stop.

Jonathan went flying out of the seat. He landed, with a thump, in the ditch.

"Jonathan, are you all right?" cried his friends.

He sat up and blinked, and rubbed his head. Then he smiled a big smile.

"It worked! The anchor worked! It stopped the car!" laughed Jonathan. "Yippeee!"

His friends looked down at him, frowning.

A Happy Day

"LET'S have a picnic by the river," said Mother Bear. "And we'll ask everybody to join us." When Father Bear and Little Richard agreed, she hurried into the kitchen to make a big picnic.

Away they drove to pick up their friends. But, oh dear, there was no one at home at Angelo's house. And Kenny Pig's store was closed. Even Miss Kitty was out. How sad!

"Now we'll have to have our picnic all alone," said Little Richard sadly.

Father Bear parked the truck and carried the picnic to the river.

"Whoopee! Here they are!" shouted Little Richard, as they ran along the bank.

Yes, there were their friends, swimming, or riding in Rabbit's gondola.

"We're just going home. Everyone's hungry," said Angelo.

"Stay where you are. I've brought a picnic," said Mother Bear.

"Hooray for Mother Bear! Now we can stay," cheered her friends. They helped her unload the big picnic and spread the cloth.

Father Bear gave Mother a kiss on the cheek. Then he did a magnificent cannonball into the river. It was a happy day.

25

The Big Parade

For weeks everybody had been getting ready for the big parade. And now it was about to start. Everyone was excited and happy. Everyone but Baby Squirrel. He clung to his Mother's skirt and cried, "I want to pway my dwum in the pawade. I WANT to!"

"But you're too little to march all the way to the river, dear," said Mother Squirrel.

"But I WANT to!" cried Baby. And he was such a little, little Squirrel that he sat down on his drum and sobbed. It was very sad.

Zippy Raccoon whispered something in Mother Squirrel's ear. Then he picked up Baby Squirrel, who clung to his drum, and carried him off.

Now what was Zippy up to? wondered the watchers. Then, suddenly, the whistle blew. "Here comes the parade!" someone cried. Oh, it was thrilling!

First came Jonathan holding the flag of River Bend. Behind him marched Kenny Pig, pounding the big drum. Rabbit tootled the bugle. And Baby Squirrel's father, Angelo Squirrel, blew the slide trombone.

Behind the band, slowly, drove Father Bear. He had decorated the truck with lovely crepe paper flowers. And sitting among them was Miss Kitty, with a crown on her head.

The cheering and clapping grew louder, for marching beside the float was Zippy Raccoon. His mail sack hung down to his middle. And in it sat Baby Squirrel, pounding his toy drum.

Goodness, he looked so proud and happy!

Three times around came the parade. And each time Baby Squirrel passed by he got the biggest cheers.

Then all the watchers joined in and marched to the river bank for a big picnic. Oh it was a glorious day! Especially for Baby Squirrel. He just managed to nibble a bit of cake when his head began to nod.

He was so sleepy from marching in his first big parade that he napped, on the grassy river bank, and dreamed it all over again.

27

Too Hot To Play

I T WAS a hot, buzzing, breathless summer day. Miss Kitty sat in her hammock under the shade tree, thinking of cool things.

Rabbit stopped on his way to the river and panted, "It's a hot day, Miss Kitty. Much too hot to play. You look nice and cool in that hammock."

"Then come and join me," said Miss Kitty.

Rabbit climbed gratefully into the hammock and rocked gently in the shade. Then Jonathan came shuffling up the path.

"It's so warm I can hardly take another step," he said.

"Then come and join us in the hammock," called Rabbit.

"Aaah! This is nice," sighed Jonathan.

Little Richard leaned his bike on the fence and joined his friends in the hammock.

"It's just too hot to play," he said. Now the hammock was sagging.

"I'm getting squished," groaned Jonathan. "Somebody move."

The Walking Hat

JONATHAN waved to Angelo, who was on his way to the dump. Then he saw something round and black and flat roll off Angelo's truck.

"Why, it's an old silk hat," said Jonathan. "The kind with the spring inside that pops up!"

He poked inside the old hat with his fishing rod to find the spring. And his hook got tangled in the hat.

"Silly hat!" muttered Jonathan, yanking hard on his rod. POP! Up popped the silk hat to its full height.

He crawled inside the hat to unhook his rod. Then his sleeve got caught on the fishing hook. Jonathan tugged and pulled, and the hat rolled over in the lane. Poor Jonathan found himself hanging inside that tall black hat by his own fishing hook.

The hat was lying quietly in the lane when Kenny came by. "That's a nice hat," he said. And he bent down for it just as the hat jumped.

"Oooh," howled Kenny, and he ran into the bushes. Then Kenny picked up a stone and flung it at the hat—BANG!

Down fell Jonathan. Then he crawled out of the hat, tired, but happy to see the sunlight again.

Little Richard moved over and the hammock swung wildly.

"Your feet are on my stomach, Rabbit," giggled miss Kitty. Rabbit leaned over the side of the hammock, almost tipping them over. Now everybody was laughing and shouting, "Ooh, stop! I'm getting dizzy!"

Soon they had the hammock swinging fast. It tipped over and tumbled them on the grass. Everybody laughed and scrambled back into the hammock, just to tip it over again.

They had so much fun tumbling out of the hammock, only to scramble in again, they all forgot it was just too hot to play on that hot, buzzing, breathless summer day.

29

Castaways

RABBIT sang a tender song as he punted his gondola down the river and out to sea. He was taking his friends to Sprite Island for a picnic. Miss Kitty trailed a paw in the water and said,

"I wish we could stay overnight and have a beach party by moonlight."

"Someday we will," promised Rabbit. "Someday when we have bedrolls and flashlights and all the supplies we need for overnight. Someday."

"Sooo-oo-omeday!" chanted Jonathan.

They moored the gondola in a little cove at the Island.

"We'll have to leave before the tide goes out too far," said Rabbit, "because the boat needs water to float."

They swam. Jonathan caught a fish. They spread the blankets and cooked their picnic on a bonfire. What fun it was to be on an island!

"I just wish we could stay all night," said Miss Kitty.

"Someday," yawned Rabbit. His head nodded. And soon he was asleep.

"Uumpph! Uumpph!" Kenny Pig snored peacefully in the sun.

Miss Kitty and Jonathan set out to explore the island. They gathered a bucketful of clams. They were so busy they forgot all about the tide. When they wandered back to their friends, Rabbit was frowning at his boat, high and dry on the sand.

"Well, we won't get off the island tonight," said Rabbit. "And here we are without a flashlight or bedrolls or food!"

Kenny Pig woke up and groaned, "Food! I'm starving!"

"Never mind, we have everything we need," said Jonathan.

They hurried to gather driftwood. As the moon rose, their great bonfire brightened the beach. They drew the blankets close to the fire and everyone was as snug as could be.

There was plenty of supper, even for Kenny. They cooked Jonathan's fish on the fire, and steamed the clams open in seaweed. It was lovely to sit around a bonfire by moonlight. They told stories and sang songs until they were all sung out.

"Thank you for the lovely beach party, Rabbit," said Miss Kitty.

"You're welcome, Miss Kitty. I promised you a moonlit beach party, someday," said Rabbit. He felt as happy as if he'd planned it all that way from the very beginning.

Two-Family House

Mr. Foxy stood on a ladder and hammered a shingle over a hole in his roof.

"There, that ought to keep those noisy squirrels out of my attic this winter," he said.

Today was moving day for Angelo's family. With a sack in each paw, they climbed the big tree that reached to that little hole.

"Well, isn't that thoughtful," smiled Angelo. "Mr. Foxy seems to be putting up a storm door for us to keep out the cold."

Mother Squirrel smiled.

"Quickly dear, run down and thank him before he goes inside."

But it was too late. Mr. Foxy had kicked the ladder down and slammed the front door behind him with a loud bang.

"Very, very thoughtful," said Angelo. "Now I'll just run along the drainpipe and open the new door for you."

But when Angelo got to the new door he had a bit of trouble.

"Mr. Foxy seems to have put it on a bit tightly," said Angelo.

"He was only thinking of our comfort, dear," said Mother. "Push!"

"I'm pushing," grunted Angelo. "Ah, there we are! He put a nail loosely in the top so we could swing the shingle back and forth."

"The dear thing," said Mother as she led her little ones into the big, warm attic. With a crash and a rattle the squirrels dumped their sacks of nuts into the closet.

Downstairs, Mr. Foxy jumped up from his chair and shouted,

"So you're back! I can hear you up there!" He banged on the ceiling with his broom.

"Hear that, Dad?" smiled Mother Squirrel. "He banged on the ceiling to welcome us back, just like old times."

Angelo and the children played a noisy game of nut-ball while Mother set the table. And downstairs, Mr. Foxy put the broom in the corner and smiled.

He'd felt a bit mean putting the shingle over the squirrels' hole. Why, come to think of it, he'd been feeling lonely lately. As he listened to the thumps upstairs it seemed cozy to hear somebody else moving about the house.

33

Harvest Day

THE morning after the first frost was Harvest Day in River Bend. Everyone in the village helped Father Bear pick the ripened apples in his orchard.

Standing on tall ladders, the bigger folk picked apples growing high in the trees, while the youngsters filled barrels with apples that had fallen to the ground. The air was sweet and tangy with the scent of apples, and noisy with jokes and songs.

Father Bear and Kenny Pig carried the big apple barrels into the barn to be stored. The barrels were heavy. All day long Kenny Pig and Father Bear had been bragging about who was the strongest. While Father Bear staggered into the barn with a huge barrel, Kenny decided to play a little joke.

He climbed into an apple barrel and hid. When Father Bear picked it up he puffed and grunted.

"Ooof! Oh my! This is a heavy one. You could never lift this one, Kenny!"

He was grunting so loudly that he didn't hear Kenny laughing inside the barrel. Everybody else was laughing too. Father Bear just kept staggering under that barrel and shouting,

"Look at this, Kenny. Ooof! Oops!" Then suddenly, he dropped the barrel. And down, down, down the hill it rolled.

"Oh my apples!" groaned Father Bear.

"Oh Kenny!" cried his friends, chasing after the barrel.

Down the hill it rolled, until SPLASH! it rolled into the pond.

Nobody was more surprised than Father Bear when Kenny bobbed up in the pond! Kenny laughed and shouted to Father Bear.

"That proves I'm the strongest. You couldn't carry me!"

Kenny didn't mind the ducking because he was so hot from carrying those barrels. He splashed and frolicked like a whale.

CLANG! CLANG! Mother Bear was ringing the dinner bell, calling her friends into the big kitchen. They were all so hungry from picking apples and chasing and playing that they could hardly wait to reach the table.

And what a feast they had! Corn on the cob, meat and mashed potatoes, hot corn muffins with melted butter! Watermelon and ice cream, apple pie and pumpkin pie. It was delicious! Everyone ate as heartily as a farm hand. And they all agreed, as they did every year, that it was the best Harvest Day ever!

Boo!

THE moon shone bright as a Jack-o'-Lantern that ghostly Halloween night. In front of Mr. Foxy's dark and haunted-looking house stood a witch and scarecrow, carrying their trick or treat bags.

"I wish something really scarey would happen," said Rabbit, the witch.

"I do, too. I'd like to meet a real ghost," said the scarecrow, who was really Little Richard.

"Mr. Foxy's house is the only one we haven't been to," said Rabbit. "But he never gives out treats on Halloween."

"Then we can play a trick on him," said Little Richard. "I know what. When he opens the door we'll shout 'BOO' and scare him."

The two spooks climbed the stairs of Mr. Foxy's house.

Creak! Creak! Creak! groaned the stairs.

"Um, maybe we shouldn't scare him," whispered Rabbit. But already Little Richard was tapping on the door.

"Let's go," whispered Rabbit, nervously. But just then, they heard something moving inside. Softly, slowly, it shuffled closer and closer to the door. Then the door handle turned with a Creeeeaaak! Slowly it opened . . .

"Bu-bub-ooh!" cried Little Richard. But the boo wouldn't come out. For there at the door stood a big, dark shape holding a candle!

"Oooooh!" it wailed, in the scariest way.

"Oh help! Run!" cried the witch and the scarecrow jumping back.

They ran down the steps, and they didn't stop until they'd flung themselves into Kenny Pig's bright, warm store.

"Oh, am I scared!" shivered Rabbit. "Mr. Foxy really tricked us!"

"M-maybe it wasn't Mr. Foxy," stuttered Little Richard. "Maybe it was a real, well . . . you know, a real ghost! I mean, it is Halloween!"

"No such thing as a ghost," said Kenny, biting into a candy apple.

Of course, his friends knew there really wasn't. But it was such great fun to be scared on Halloween!

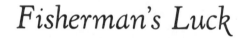

Fisherman's Luck

ICE formed on the river like bits of shattered glass. Jonathan felt cold and discouraged. He was having trouble catching a fish.

A big, gray seagull was fishing there too. The gull plunged noisily into the river, frightening the fish away. Jonathan was just about to pack up for home when he felt a tug on his line. He pulled on his pole, and out of the water flew a big fish.

"What luck!" laughed Jonathan.

But the gray gull swooped low and snapped up the fish with its beak.

"Now see here!" shouted Jonathan, pulling on his pole.

The wicked seagull flew away, carrying the fish and the pole, and Jonathan.

It was a funny sight, as poor Jonathan clung to his pole and sailed over the river, shouting angrily at the gull.

As it flew over Miss Kitty's roof the gull snapped his beak shut and swallowed the fish! Down, down fell Jonathan. Down into the chimney!

Miss Kitty was sweeping the floor when she heard a rackety-CRASH! Cinders billowed from the fireplace in a great black cloud.

"Help!" squealed Miss Kitty.

When the soot had cleared away Jonathan was sitting in the fireplace. He was so sooty that all you could see were his round eyes and his teeth. He was laughing.

"Well, Jonathan Mouse. Why didn't you come in the front door the way you always do?" asked Miss Kitty crisply.

That made Jonathan laugh even harder. "Because, haha! Oh. Ho! Ho! You see, Miss Kitty, you've always told me to, haha! to just drop in! So I did!"

First Snowfall

ALL night long the snow had fallen, thick as powdered sugar. "You should see Big Meadow, it's just perfect for sleigh-riding!" said Rabbit. "If we only had a sleigh!"

"If only we had a sleigh!" echoed Jonathan.

"Maybe Kenny has one," said Miss Kitty, as the three friends trudged along Shady Lane.

Outside the store they found poor Kenny working hard. A big barrel had broken, spilling potatoes all over the lane.

"We'll help you," called his friends. And they hurried to gather the potatoes out of the snow. With everyone helping, Kenny's potatoes were soon piled into baskets, safely inside the store.

"Now if you have a sleigh, Kenny, we can all go sleigh-riding," said Rabbit.

"Oh I haven't," said Kenny. "I've always meant to make one."

Suddenly everybody felt very sad, as they thought of Big Meadow, slick and fast with snow.

"How would you make one?" asked Rabbit.

"Well, let's see," said Kenny, sitting himself down on a long wooden box. "I'd take some side pieces from a wooden barrel. You see,

they're rounded, and they would make the runners. And then . . ."

"And then . . ." interrupted Miss Kitty, clapping her mittens with excitement, ". . . and then you could take that big box you're sitting on and hammer it to the barrel staves, to make the seat!"

Everyone ran outside the store to look at the broken barrel.

They got right to work taking the barrel to pieces. They found a hammer and nails on Kenny's hardware shelf. And soon the box was sitting trimly on top of the barrel staves.

"Oh it's a beautiful sleigh!" said Miss Kitty, standing inside the box. Rabbit was busy tying a long rope to the front of it.

"And to think I was going to chop up that barrel for firewood!" said Kenny Pig.

Off they went to the top of Big Meadow, pulling Miss Kitty and Jonathan in the sleigh. Then they climbed inside. Kenny pushed.

And down the hill they raced, lickety-split, to the bottom! Oh it was fun! Up and down, up and down they rode, all day long. For Rabbit was right. Big Meadow was just perfect for sleigh-riding.

41

Lost and Found

Baby Squirrel could not learn to make his bed. Mother Squirrel had shown him how to pull up the sheet and blankets and pat them smooth, then put the pillow neatly on top. But Baby Squirrel always forgot.

In the morning he would wake up his dolly, which was an old stuffed sock. They would play all day. And at bedtime, Baby put his dolly back into his unmade bed.

"Christmas is coming, and Santa Claus likes good little squirrels who make their beds," said Father Angelo as he tucked him in.

But Baby could never remember.

One morning Baby Squirrel woke up and found that his dolly was not in bed beside him. Baby looked under the bed. No dolly. He hunted down inside his bed. No dolly there.

He pulled up the sheet and looked under the blanket. No. Dolly wasn't there. He pulled up the blanket and patted it, hoping to find a lump. And dolly wasn't hiding under the pillow, for Baby shook it, and dropped it on the bed.

Oh dear. Where could his dolly be? Baby was just about to cry and run for help when he saw his doll sitting on the dresser!

Baby caught up his doll and hugged him and spanked him for hiding that way. Just then, Mother Squirrel opened the door and cried,

"Why Baby, you've made your bed!" She was so happy and so surprised! Baby Squirrel was surprised too. Mother kissed him and said,

"Now we can tell Santa you're a good little squirrel who makes his bed."

And that made Baby happy all over again.

42

"Then I have toys for you all!" Santa was just about to open his toy sack when the front door opened. A merry voice laughed,

"Ho! Ho! Ho!" and another Santa Claus backed into the room! He was backing in, because his beard was caught on the door handle. The elastic snapped. ZING! His beard flew across the room.

"Ho! Ho! Ho!" laughed the first Santa. "And who are you?"

"I'm Santa Claus," grinned Father Bear. Now everyone was very puzzled. If Father Bear was Santa, who could the other one be?

Baby Squirrel climbed on Santa's lap and tugged at his beard.

"Ouch!" roared Santa.

Then Baby flung his paws around Santa's neck, and all the little ones climbed onto his lap to hug him and cheer,

The Unexpected Guest

It was Christmas Eve, and all of Miss Kitty's friends were gathered about her glittering tree.

"It's almost time for Santa to come in the door," said Rabbit.

The little ones squealed with excitement. Of course, everyone knew it was really Father Bear dressed up as Santa, but they loved to pretend.

Suddenly there was a rattle in the chimney and a thump on the hearth. And there was a jolly Santa Claus striding into the room laughing, "Ho! Ho! Ho!" He dropped his toy sack to the floor.

"Now how did Father Bear ever climb down the chimney?" they wondered. He'd never looked so Santa-Clausey before!

"Merry Christmas! Merry Christmas! Have you all been good?" asked Santa Claus.

"Yes, Santa," called the little ones.

43

"It's really Santa Claus! It's really him!"

"Yes, it's really me. I've flown all over the world tonight, and I just stopped by to wish you all a Merry Christmas," said Santa Claus.

Miss Kitty brought him a cup of cocoa. Then Santa opened his toy sack and gave each of his friends a lovely present. There were toys and games and shawls and hats. For Santa knew just what each one wanted.

Then dear Santa said, "It's time to go, for Mrs. Claus is waiting."

With a last "Merry Christmas!" he whisked up the chimney. Then everyone hurried into the snow. With a clatter of hoofs, Santa's reindeer leapt off the roof. Santa waved, and a shower of sparks tumbled from the runners of his sleigh.

"Merry Christmas, Santa! Come to our party next year in River Bend!"

With their hearts filled with joy, his friends waved until Santa's sleigh disappeared far, far off in the starry sky.

About the Author

Patricia Scarry, who divides her time between Switzerland, France, and Nantucket Island, is the author of numerous heartwarming books for children. The wife of popular children's book author/illustrator Richard Scarry and the mother of Huck Scarry, also an author/illustrator of children's books, Mrs. Scarry is adept at creating everyday adventures that children want to read again and again. Among her best-known books are *Patricia Scarry's Little Willy and Spike, The Sweet Smell of Christmas,* and *Patsy Scarry's Big Bedtime Storybook.*

About the Illustrator

Tibor Gergely, the award-winning illustrator of more than 50 beloved books for children, was a self-taught artist who brought the warmth and vitality of his eastern European childhood to his works. Tibor Gergely's inspiring illustrations graced the pages of numerous Golden Books, such as *The Little Red Caboose, Scuffy the Tugboat, The Taxi That Hurried, Tootle,* and *The Happy Man and His Dump Truck.*